Enid Blyton

Enid Blyton was born in London in 1897. Her childhood was spent in Beckenham, Kent, and as a child she began to write poems, stories and plays. She trained to be a teacher but it was as a children's author to which she devoted her whole life. Her first book was a collection of poems for children, published in 1922. In 1926 she began to write a weekly magazine for children called *Sunny Stories,* and it was here that many of her most popular stories and characters first appeared. The magazine was immensely popular and in 1953 it became *The Enid Blyton Magazine.*

She wrote more than 600 books for children and many of her most popular series are still published all over the world. Her books have been translated into over 30 languages. Enid Blyton died in 1968.

Enid Blyton's

WHISKERS FOR THE CAT

and other stories

Illustrated by
Paul Crompton, Edgar Hodges
and Joyce Johnson

Cliveden Press

Contents

Whiskers for the cat	7
The spelling spell	16
The quarrelsome bears	29
Roll around, Brer Rabbit	36
Bing-Bong, the paw-reader	45
Millicent Mary's surprise	63
The cat who flew away	70
The Gossamer Elf	79
The day the Princess came	88
Mollie's mud-pies	105
Brer Rabbit goes fishing	117
The bonnet dame	124

Whiskers for the cat

In the corner of the playroom there was a small rocking horse. He was only half the usual size, but the smaller children liked him because he just fitted them nicely.

He had big rockers and he creaked a little when the children rode him. "*Cree-eek, cree-eek,*" he said. And the toys got quite used to the noise.

"I'm the only toy in this playroom big enough for the children to ride on," boasted the little rocking horse. "I ought to be King of the playroom."

"Well, you won't be," said the curly-haired doll. "You squashed the monkey's tail yesterday, and that was unkind."

"I didn't mean to," said the horse, offended. "He shouldn't have left it lying about under my rockers. Silly of him."

"You should have looked down before you began to rock, and you would have seen it," said the doll.

"Well, do you suppose I'm going to bother to look for tails and things before I begin to rock?" said the horse. "You just look out for yourselves! That's the best thing to do."

But the toys were careless. Once the little red toy motor car ran under the horse's rockers, and was squashed

almost flat. And another time the clockwork clown left his key there and the rocking horse bent it when he rocked on it. It was difficult to wind up the clown after that, and he was cross.

Then the baby doll dropped her bead necklace and the rocking horse rocked on it and smashed the beads. The toys were really very angry with him about that.

"Why did you rock just then? Only because you knew you would break the beads!" they cried. "You are really very unkind. We shan't speak to you or play with you."

"Don't then," said the horse, and he rocked away by himself. *"Cree-eek, creek-eek!* I'm sure I don't want to talk to you *or* give you rides if you are so cross and silly."

After that nobody took any notice of the little rocking horse. The worst of it was that Johnny, the little boy who often rode him, went away to stay with his granny for a long time, so nobody rode the horse at all. It was very dull for him.

"I wish they'd talk to me!" thought the horse sadly. "I wish they'd play. I'd like to give them each a ride – in fact, I'd take three of them at once if they asked me."

But the toys acted as if the rocking horse wasn't there at all. They didn't ask him anything. They didn't even look at him.

"He's unkind and selfish and horrid," they said. "And the best way to treat people like that is not to take any notice of them."

So the rocking horse got duller and duller, and he longed to gallop round the playroom just for a change. But he was afraid the toys might be cross if he did.

Now one day the puppy came into the playroom, because someone had left the door open. The toys fled to the toy cupboard in fear, because the puppy was very playful and liked to carry a toy outside and chew it.

Everyone got safely into the cupboard except the black cat. She slipped and fell, and the puppy pounced on her. He chewed her black head and nibbled her whiskers away. Nobody dared to rescue her, not even the rocking horse, though he did wonder if he should gallop at the puppy.

Then somebody whistled and the puppy flew out of the door and downstairs. The poor black cat sat up. "My head does feel chewed!" she said. "And oh – what's happened to my fine black whiskers?"

"They've gone," said the teddy bear, peeping out of the cupboard. "The puppy has chewed them off. There they are, look, on the floor, in tiny little bits."

The black cat cried bitterly. She had been proud of her whiskers. "A cat doesn't look like a cat without her whiskers," she wept. "What shall I do? Can I get any more?"

Well, the toys did try their very hardest to get her some whiskers, but there were none to be found anywhere. And then a humble voice came from the corner where the little rocking horse stood.

"Excuse me, toys – but I've got an idea."

"It's only the rocking horse," said the teddy bear. "Don't take any notice of him."

"Please do take some notice," said the horse. "I've got a *good* idea. I should be very pleased to give the toy cat some of the hairs out of my long white tail. They would do beautifully for whiskers."

There was a silence after this. Then the toy cat stood up. "Well! That's a very good idea indeed, and *very* kind of you!" she said, and she walked over to the horse. "But how can I get some hairs from your tail?"

"Pull them out, of course," said the horse.

"But it will hurt you," said the toy cat.

"I don't mind," said the horse, bravely, "pull as many as you like!" So the toy cat pulled seven out, and they did hurt. But the horse didn't make a sound.

Then the curly-haired doll threaded a big needle with one of the hairs and ran it gently through the toy cat's cheeks. "One whisker!" she said. She threaded the needle again. "Two whiskers! Three whiskers! Oh, you will look fine, Toy Cat. These are white whiskers, long and strong, and you will look very, very beautiful now."

"I must say it was nice of the rocking horse to give you them," said the teddy bear, suddenly. "Especially as we haven't even spoken to him lately. Very nice of him."

Everyone thought the same. So when the toy cat's new whiskers were all in place, and she looked very fine indeed, the toys went with her to show her to the rocking horse.

"Very good idea of yours!" said the curly-haired doll.

"Very kind of you," said the teddy bear.

"I can't thank you enough!" said the black cat. "I had black whiskers before, and they didn't show up very well – but these show beautifully. Don't you think so?"

"You look lovely," said the horse. "Very lovely."

"Your tail looks a bit thin now, I'm afraid," said the toy cat. "Do you mind?"

"Not a bit," said the rocking horse. "I can rock to and fro just as fast when my tail is thin as when it's thick. You get on my back and see, Black Cat!"

So up got the black cat, and the rocking horse went rocking round the playroom at top speed. It was very exciting. You may be sure the horse looked where he was going! He wasn't going to rock over anyone's tail again!

"Oh, thank you!" said the toy cat, quite out of breath. "That was the nicest ride I ever had!"

"Anyone can have one!" said the

horse, rather gruffly, because he was afraid that the toys might say 'No', and turn their backs on him.

But they didn't. They all climbed up at once. "Nice old horse!" they said. "We're friends again now, aren't we? Gallop away, gallop away!"

And you should have seen him gallop away again.

The spelling spell

Once Mr Stamp-About went through Dimity Wood in a great rage. He stamped as he went and muttered to himself, and he even shook his fist in the air.

"I'll pay old Snorty back for not giving me what he owes me! How am I to pay *my* bills if he doesn't pay his? How dare he say that the apples I sold him were bad, and not worth a penny! How *dare* he not pay me for them!"

The rabbits ran away from his stamping feet, and the squirrels bounded up into the trees. The robin followed him, flying from tree to tree in wonder. What was the matter now with noisy old Stamp-About?

Stamp-About didn't notice that he had taken the wrong path in the wood. He went on and on, and then suddenly found that the path was getting very narrow. He stopped and looked round.

"I've taken the wrong path! All because of Snorty! I am so angry with him that I don't even see the way I am walking!"

He stood there a few moments, wondering what to do. "Perhaps there's someone nearby who will hear me if I shout, and tell me the right path," he thought. So he gave a loud shout. "Ho there! I want help!"

Nobody answered at all, and the birds all flew away in fright, for Stamp-About had such a tremendous voice! He yelled again. "Ho there! I want help!"

And this time a voice called back to him – a very cross voice indeed.

"Will you be quiet? You're spoiling

my spell!"

Stamp-About could hardly believe his ears. Spoiling someone's spell? Whose? And if the someone was near enough to shout back, why didn't he come to help Stamp-About? "Rude fellow!" thought Stamp-About, angrily. "I'll go and tell him what I think of him!"

So he pushed his way fiercely through the bushes and came to a little clearing, set neatly round with red-spotted toadstools in a ring. In the middle sat a little fellow in a long black cloak that shimmered like moonlight. He had two long feelers on his forehead, just like a butterfly.

In front of him a small fire burnt, and on it was a clear bowl of glass, which, strangely enough, seemed not to mind the flames at all.

"Why didn't you come to help me?" stormed Stamp-About.

"Please go away," said the little fellow, turning round. "Yelling like that in my spell time, I never heard of such a thing! Go and buy yourself a few manners!"

Stamp-About almost exploded with temper. "How dare you," he cried. "Who are you, you — you miserable, uncivil little fellow!"

"I'm Weeny, the little wizard," said the small man. "And I get my living by making spells at this time each day and selling them. And then *you* come blustering along and spoil them all. Just when I was making gold, too! Pah!"

"*Gold?*" said Stamp-About, in quite a different voice. "Good gracious — can you make *gold?*"

"Not exactly," said the little wizard. "But my spells can! I've only to pop the right things into my little glass bowl here, and spell each one as they dissolve — and at the end what do I find? A handful of gold at the bottom of my bowl!"

"*Really?*" said Stamp-About, wishing he hadn't been rude. "Er — I'm sorry I disturbed you. Please start all over again! But why do you have to *spell* each word – why can't you just *say* it?"

"Don't be silly," said the little wizard. "A spell is a spell because it's *spelt*, isn't it? You can't make a spell unless you spell it, can you?"

"I don't know," said Stamp-About, and he came into the toadstool ring, treading on one as he did so.

"Get out!" said the wizard, pointing a long thin finger at him. "Treading on my magic toadstool! Get out! I'll turn you into a worm and call down that robin over there to eat you if you're not careful!"

Stamp-About hurriedly stepped out of the ring of toadstools, being very careful not to break one again.

"Now go away, and let me start my gold spell all over again," commanded the fierce little fellow.

Stamp-About tiptoed away, and hid behind a tree. All right – let the wizard order him about all he liked – he would hide and watch the spell and then *he* would make it too, when he got home! Aha – gold for the making – what a wonderful thing!

He peeped from behind a tree and watched. The wizard took no more notice of him. He had a pile of things to put into the glass bowl – but first he poured into it some water from a little jug.

Then he took a buttercup and shredded its golden petals one by one into the bowl, muttering as he did so. Stamp-About strained his ears, but he couldn't catch what was being said, until he heard the wizard say, "C-U-P."

"Of course – he's only *spelling* the name of the flower!" thought Stamp-About. "Now – what's he putting in this time? Oh – one of the red toadstools. And now he's spelling that. Ho – what an easy spell to make!"

He watched carefully. The little wizard took another buttercup and spelt out its name – then he took a

twig of hawthorn blossom and shook the white petals into the bowl, and then another buttercup.

"He's spelling everything," thought Stamp-About. "Well, who would have thought that *spelling* had anything to do with the making of spells? This is going to be very useful to me! What is he taking now?"

The wizard had picked up the empty shell of a robin's egg and had crushed it up and dropped it into the bubbling water, which was a bright mixture of colours. He muttered as he spelt the name, and then threw in yet another shower of buttercup petals.

Then he danced lightly round the bowl three times and stopped. To Stamp-About's astonishment all the water in the bowl rose up as a cloud of steam — leaving a gleaming handful of gold at the bottom of the bowl!

"Look at that," whispered Stamp-About to himself in glee, as he watched the wizard put the gold into a wallet. "Now I know exactly how to make the spell. I'll go home and do it."

The little wizard took up the bowl, put it into a small bag, and then he stamped out the fire. He disappeared like a shadow through the trees.

"I'll follow him," thought Stamp-About. "He must know the way out of this wood."

So he followed carefully, and soon came to a path he knew. He went one way and the little wizard went the other. Stamp-About was so excited that he went home smiling all over his face – much to the surprise of Snorty, who was leaning over his gate as Stamp-About passed.

"You're in a better temper now, are you?" called Snorty. "Well, perhaps now you'll admit that those apples of yours *were* bad – and that I don't owe you for them after all!"

"I don't need a penny from you, Snorty, not a penny!" said Stamp-About. "I shall soon be rich. I shall pay all the bills I owe – and you'll come borrowing from *me*, you see if you don't!"

Well, this was very astonishing news to Snorty, who soon spread it about that Stamp-About was going to be rich.

"How?" asked his friends. "What's he going to do? Let's go round and ask him."

When they came to Stamp-About's house he was out in his garden. He had made a small fire in the middle of the lawn, and on it he had placed a little glass bowl – the one in which his goldfish once used to swim.

"Look at that," said Snorty in amazement. "What's he doing? See – he's got a pile of queer things beside him – buttercups – a red toadstool – and what's that – the shell of an egg? And look, there's a spray of hawthorn blossom too, off the may hedge."

Stamp-About saw everyone watching and was very pleased to show off. He did exactly as he had seen the little wizard do – first he threw in the buttercup petals, shredding them off the flower head one by one. As he did so, he spelt the name out loud in a high chanting voice.

"B-u-t-e-r-c-u-p!"

Then he took up the red toadstool and put that into the bowl of water too. Again he chanted out loud, spelling the name clearly.

"R-e-d t-o-a-d-s-t-o-o-l!"

Then he shredded buttercup petals again and spelt the name as before, and then took the hawthorn blossom.

"H-o-r-t-h-o-r-n!"

And in went the white may petals as he shook the twig over the bowl! Aha – the water was changing colour now. Soon the handful of gold would come!

In went more buttercup petals and the name was spelt: "B-u-t-e-r-c-u-p!"

Then he dropped in the broken shell of a robin's egg. As he crumpled up the shell and it fell into the water Stamp-About spelt out the name in a loud voice. "R-o-b-b-i-n's e-g-g!"

And last of all another shower of golden buttercup petals went into the bubbling water.

Eagerly Stamp-About leaned over it. Now for the gold! First the water would disappear in a cloud of steam

– and then he would see the handful of gold at the bottom of the bowl!

But wait – first he must dance three times round the bowl!

Everyone crept forward to see what was about to happen. A cloud of steam shot high into the air and the water in the bowl disappeared. Then the bowl itself exploded with such a bang that everyone fell over backwards.

Stamp-About sat down very suddenly indeed, scared almost out of his wits. Then he looked eagerly at the fire – had the gold been scattered about all round it?

No – there wasn't a single piece of gold. The fire had gone out when the bowl exploded, and now only one thing lay there – a large book!

"What's happened?" shouted Stamp-About in a rage. "The spell's gone wrong! It should have made gold, not a stupid book. What book is it?"

He took it up and opened it – then he looked up in astonishment and everyone crowded round to see what it was.

"It's a *dictionary*!" said Snorty, and gave a huge guffaw. "Ha ha, ho ho, I'm not surprised."

"But – why did the spell go wrong?" cried Stamp-About, and dashed the book to the ground. "I don't want a *dictionary*!"

"Yes, you do!" chuckled Snorty. "The spell went wrong because your *spelling* went wrong! Spells have to be spelled correctly! That's why all you've got is a dictionary – to help you to spell. Oh, what a joke! Can you spell 'rotten apples', Stamp-About? Oh, what a comical thing! He tried to make a spell – but he couldn't even *spell*!"

It was quite true. The spell couldn't work unless everything was spelled out correctly – and Stamp-About had conjured up something he needed as much as gold: a dictionary. Poor old Stamp-About, he hasn't paid his bills *yet*!

The quarrelsome bears

There were once two bears who lived in a little yellow cottage in Toy Village. Teddy was a brown bear and Bruiny was a blue one. And how they quarrelled! Really, you should have heard them!

"That's my handkerchief you are using!" said Teddy.

"Indeed it's not!" said Bruiny.

"I tell you it *is*," said Teddy.

"And I tell you it's not!" said Bruiny.

"Don't keep telling me fibs," said Teddy.

"Well, don't you either," said Bruiny.

That was the sort of quarrel they had every single day. Silly, wasn't it? Especially as they both had more handkerchiefs than they needed.

One afternoon they dressed themselves in their best coats and ties to go to a party. They did look nice. Teddy tied Bruiny's bow and Bruiny tied Teddy's. Then they took their new hats and went to the door.

And it was raining! Not just raining quietly, but coming down angrily and fiercely—pitterpatterpitterpatterpitterpatter, without a single stop.

"Goodness! Look at that!" said Teddy. "We must take our umbrella."

They had a big red umbrella between them, and it was really a very fine one indeed. Teddy looked for it in the umbrella-stand. It wasn't there.

"What have you done with the umbrella, Bruiny?" asked Teddy.

"Nothing at all," said Bruiny, at once. "What do you suppose I've done with it? Used it to stir my tea with?"

"Don't be silly," said Teddy. "That umbrella was there yesterday. You must have taken it out."

"I did not," said Bruiny. "You must have taken it yourself."

"I haven't been out for two days," said Teddy. "What do you think I'd want with an umbrella indoors?"

"Oh, you might use it to smack the cat with," said Bruiny unkindly.

"Oh! As if I would smack our dear old cat with an umbrella!" cried Teddy angrily.

"Well – perhaps you used it to poke the fire," said Bruiny.

"And perhaps *you* used it to scrub the floor!" cried Teddy. "I can think of silly things too. No, it's no good, Bruiny. You took that umbrella for something, and you might just as well try and remember what you did with it and where you put it. Hurry, now, or we'll be late for the party."

"I tell you, Teddy, I haven't had the umbrella and I don't know where it is," said Bruiny. "It would be a good thing if *you* thought a little and found out where you had hidden it."

"I don't hide umbrellas," said Teddy.

"Well, you once hid the cat in the cupboard and it jumped out at me," said Bruiny.

"That was just a joke," said Teddy. "I shouldn't hide our umbrella in the cupboard, because it wouldn't jump out at you."

"But you'd like it to, I suppose?" cried Bruiny, getting crosser and crosser.

"Yes, I'd love to see an umbrella jump out at you!" shouted Teddy, getting angry too.

"You're a bad teddy bear!" said Bruiny, and he pulled Teddy's bow undone.

"Don't!" cried Teddy. He caught hold of Bruiny's coat, meaning to give him a good shaking. But he shook too hard and the coat tore in half!

"Oh! Oh! Look at that!" wailed Bruiny. "I'll jump on your hat for tearing my coat!"

And before Teddy could stop him, Bruiny had thrown his new hat on the floor and jumped on it. It was quite spoilt!

Then they both went mad. They tore each other's ties off. They threw both hats out of the window. They even threw each other's handkerchiefs into the waste-paper basket!

And in the middle of all this there came a knocking at the door! Bruiny went to open it, panting and torn. Outside stood Mrs Field-Mouse with all her little family. They were on their way to the party, each mouse under its own tiny umbrella.

"Goodness me! What's all the noise about?" asked Mrs Field-Mouse severely. "I knocked three times before you heard me."

"Well, Mrs Field-Mouse," said Bruiny, "Teddy has taken our umbrella and doesn't know where he put it."

"Oh, you fibber!" cried Teddy. "It's Bruiny that must have taken it, Mrs Field-Mouse. We've only got one, and it's raining, and we wanted it to go to the party."

"Dear me!" said Mrs Field-Mouse.

"What have *you* come for?" asked Bruiny.

"Well, I came to give you back your big red umbrella," said Mrs Field-Mouse with a laugh. "I suppose you forgot that you both kindly said I might have it yesterday to go home with my little family, because it was big enough to shelter them all. I promised to bring it back today. Here it is. I'm sorry you should have quarrelled about it."

She stood it in the hall-stand and then went off to the party with her little family. How they squealed when they heard the joke!

"Well, I never," said Bruiny, looking at the umbrella. "So you didn't take it, Teddy."

"And you didn't either," said Teddy. "Oh dear, how silly we are! We've got our umbrella – but we've torn our suits and ties and spoilt our hats, so we can't possibly go to the party after all."

"I beg your pardon, Teddy," said Bruiny in a small voice. "I'll make you some cocoa for tea."

"And I beg your pardon, too," said Teddy. "I'll make you some toast for tea. We'll never quarrel again!"

But they did quarrel, and do you know why? It was because Teddy couldn't find the toasting-fork, so he toasted the bread on the end of the red umbrella! Bruiny was so angry, because he said the toast tasted of mud!

Well, well, well! You can't please everybody, can you?

Roll around, Brer Rabbit

Now once Brer Rabbit learnt a new trick, and a most annoying one it was. He found out how to put his hind legs round his neck, and hold the back of his knees with his front paws. And then, having made himself into a kind of ball, he taught himself to roll along as fast as a leaf blowing in the wind!

So it happened that Brer Fox got bowled over one morning by something that hit him, *ker-blam*, on the back of his legs and laid him flat.

And then Brer Bear saw something peculiar coming towards him, rolling over and over, and he tried to get out of the way. But the strange ball hit him on his ankles and down he went!

And bless us all if it didn't happen to Brer Wolf too! Something rolled at him at top speed, tripped him up and there he was with his face in the mud, wondering what had hit him.

Now, Brer Rabbit rolled along so quickly that nobody could make out what he was, and before they could find out they were flat on the ground. Nobody *would* have found out if Brer Rabbit hadn't given himself away.

He knocked Brer Possum over, and Brer Possum fell into a holly bush and yelled the place down. Brer Rabbit almost burst himself with laughing, and he just *had* to unroll himself or he would have split his sides. He leaned against a tree and laughed.

Brer Possum heard him. He had picked himself up from the holly bush and had looked cautiously round to see what had hit him – and there, not far off, he saw Brer Rabbit holding on to a tree and laughing as loudly as a green woodpecker. And then he saw

Brer Rabbit suddenly curl himself up into a ball again, legs round his neck, and go rolling off through the wood to find someone else to bump into.

Brer Possum was very angry. He went to find Brer Bear and told him. Then they found Brer Wolf and Brer Fox and told them, too. They were all very angry with Brer Rabbit.

They tried to curl themselves up and roll too, but they couldn't. They managed to tie themselves into all kinds of knots, but somehow they couldn't manage to roll along.

"We'll have to stop this new trick of Brer Rabbit's," said Brer Fox. "It's most disrespectful of him to roll along the paths and knock us down without so much as a 'pardon me, let me pass'!"

"We'll lie in wait for him," said Brer Wolf. "You know that little glade over yonder? Well, he often comes to wash himself there, sitting in the sun and pulling first one ear down to wash and then the other. We could catch him there — and that would be the end of him!"

"Tomorrow, then," said Brer Bear, and they all agreed.

So the next day, before Brer Rabbit came along to wash his ears in the sunshine, Brer Possum, Brer Bear, Brer Fox and Brer Wolf were all in hiding behind the bushes. They waited and they waited.

Pretty soon Brer Rabbit came, rolling himself along merrily, so that it was a marvel to see him. He stood up when he came to the tree-stump, and perched himself there, humming a jolly little song.

And then Brer Bear and the others showed themselves all at once! Brer Rabbit didn't much like the look of them, but he called out, "Howdy, folks!" just as cheerfully as ever.

"You come along with us, Brer Rabbit," said Brer Wolf, with a growl.

"I'm busy," said Brer Rabbit, looking round for an escape and not seeing any.

"Busy or not, you come along with us," said Brer Fox, coming nearer.

"What's all this about?" said Brer Rabbit, pretending to be surprised.

"We're tired of that new trick of yours," said Brer Bear. "Knocking us flat like that! You ought to be ashamed of yourself, Brer Rabbit, at your age."

"I don't know my age," said Brer Rabbit, not getting off the tree-stump. "But if it's my rolling trick you're jealous of, I'd be pleased to show you how I do it."

Well, Brer Bear, Brer Possum, Brer Wolf and Brer Fox all felt they would certainly like to learn the trick. So they looked at one another, and nodded.

"Now you listen to us, Brer Rabbit," said Brer Fox. "You can show us how to do that trick, and then you're coming along with us, do you hear?"

"I hear all right," said Brer Rabbit, jumping down from the tree-stump.

"Wait," said Brer Bear hastily, afraid that Brer Rabbit would roll straight at them one after another and knock them all flat. "Wait! We're all getting behind trees to watch. So don't think you're going to do anything funny, Brer Rabbit."

"I wouldn't dream of it," said Brer Rabbit, and he rolled himself up into a ball. "Tell me when to go, and I'll roll at top speed! You're all round me, so I can't escape. You just watch and you'll see how it's done!"

"Go!" yelled all the creatures, at the tops of their voices from behind their trees.

And Brer Rabbit went. He rolled here and he rolled there, he rolled up the path and back again, and it was a wonderful sight to see him. Then he rolled right into a bramble bush, and Brer Possum squealed with laughter, because he knew how prickly a bramble bush was.

Brer Rabbit didn't come out of the bush. "He's hurt himself on the prickles," said Brer Possum, with another squeal of laughter. "He's got stuck there!"

They all went to see. But there was no Brer Rabbit in the bramble bush at all. Not a sign of him!

And then Brer Bear suddenly saw something – a big rabbit-hole in the middle of the bush! Aha! Old Brer Rabbit knew that hole well! He used it many a time when he wanted to – and he had certainly wanted to that morning!

He had just rolled right up to it – and then rolled right down it, much to the amazement of a small cousin of his who was on the way up! What a thing to do!

Brer Possum, Brer Bear, Brer Fox and Brer Wolf stood round the bramble bush and gazed angrily at the hole. "He's gone!" said Brer Bear. "We shan't see Brer Rabbit for a month of Sundays now!"

And then something hit them from behind, *ker-blam, ker-plunk*, and they all shot into the bramble bush on their faces. When they got up, there was nothing to be seen.

"If that was Brer Rabbit rolling up on us from behind again, I'll – I'll – I'll pull all his whiskers off!" spluttered Brer Bear.

It was, of course. He had rolled down the hole, out at the other end, and come back to see where the others were. One more roll and they were in the bramble bush!

There's no doing anything with old Brer Rabbit – he's worse than a bagful of monkeys!

Bing-Bong, the paw-reader

Flip and Binkle had been good for a week and three days, and Binkle was beginning to find things very dull.

"Oh!" he groaned, "can't we find a more exciting job than delivering medicine for Sammy Squirrel the chemist? I hate carrying baskets of bottles every day."

Flip preferred to be good. He was afraid of Binkle's exciting ideas; they nearly always led to trouble.

"It's a *very nice* job," he said anxiously. "For goodness sake don't give it up, Binkle."

Binkle put on his cap and opened the door of their home, Heather Cottage.

"Come on!" he said crossly. "I won't

give up the job – not until we get a better one, anyway!"

The two rabbits ran across Bumble Bee Common on their way to Oak Tree Town. When they got there, Binkle saw a big notice pinned up outside Dilly Duck's at the Post Office. He crossed over to look at it. In big letters it said:

A GRAND BAZAAR
WILL BE HELD IN
OAK TREE TOWN

Binkle stroked his fine whiskers and began thinking.

"Come on," said Flip, pulling him next door into Sammy Squirrel's. "Don't dream like that, Binkle. It's time we began work."

But all that day Binkle went on thinking, and hardly said a single word to Flip. In the evening, when Sammy Squirrel paid him, Binkle gave Flip a dreadful shock.

"We shan't be here tomorrow," he said, "so I'm afraid you must get someone else to do the job."

"Oh, Binkle!" cried Flip in dismay. "Whatever do you mean?"

"Sh! I've got a lovely idea!" said Binkle, pulling Flip outside. "Come on, and I'll talk to you about it."

"I don't like your lovely ideas," wailed Flip.

"You'll love this one," said Binkle. "Listen. Did you read that notice about the Bazaar outside Dilly Duck's?"

"Yes," said Flip. "What about it?"

"Well, at the Bazaar there's going to be Bing-Bong, who can read all your life in your paw," said Binkle excitedly. "He'll tell you what's going to happen to you in the future, too."

"Bing-Bong! I never heard of *him*," said Flip. "Anyway, what's it to do with us?"

"Oh, Flip, *can't you guess? One of us will be Bing-Bong*, and read everyone's paws!" said Binkle excitedly.

"Binkle! How can you be so silly?" gasped Flip. "You *know* we can't read paws!"

"Well, we don't need to, silly!" grinned Binkle. "We know all about everyone in Oak Tree Town, don't we? And we can easily tell them all about themselves. They won't know us, for we'll be dressed up, and they'll think we're wonderful!"

"But how can we tell them what will happen in the future?" asked Flip.

"We'll make it up!" said Binkle. "Oh, Flip, what fun it will be!"

"Will it?" said Flip doubtfully. "But look here, Binkle – you're to be Bing-Bong. I don't look a bit like a Bing-Bong person. You do, you're so fat and big, and you've got such lovely whiskers."

Binkle twirled them proudly.

"Yes, I shall be Bing-Bong," he said, "and you can be my assistant. First I must write a note to Herbert Hedgehog, who's putting on the Bazaar."

He sat down and got pen and paper. Presently he showed a letter to Flip. This is what it said:

BING-BONG CASTLE

Dear Sir,

I am Bing-Bong, the reader of paws. I am passing through Oak Tree Town on the day your Bazaar is held. I will call there and read paws.

Yours faithfully,
Bing-Bong.

"There!" said Binkle proudly. "What do you think of that?"

Flip's nose went nervously up and down as he read the letter.

"I *do* hope it will be all right!" he sighed. "You do have such extraordinary ideas, Binkle. I don't know how you think of them."

The letter was sent, and when it reached Herbert Hedgehog he was most excited. He at once arranged to have a little room set apart in Oak Tree Town

Hall for Bing-Bong to sit in and read paws.

"It *will* be grand," he said. "Lots of people will come to the Bazaar now!"

Binkle and Flip were very busy making clothes to wear. Binkle wore a purple suit with a red cloak wound tightly round him. On his head he wore a pointed hat with red stars painted all over it. He looked very grand.

Flip was dressed in baggy trousers and a little black velvet coat. He didn't like them much, for he felt he looked rather silly.

At last the day came, and the two rogues set out over Bumble Bee Common.

"Now remember," said Binkle, "call me Your Highness, and bow before you speak, Flip. You take the money and keep it safe. Leave the rest to me."

Flip wished he could leave *everything* to Binkle, and not go at all, but he didn't dare to say so.

"Oh my! There's Herbert Hedgehog waiting to greet us outside the Town Hall!" he whispered. "Do you think he'll see through our disguise, and know it's us?"

"Of course not!" snapped Binkle, striding forward. Herbert Hedgehog bowed very low when he saw the red-cloaked visitor.

"This is His Royal Highness Bing-Bong!" stammered Flip nervously.

Herbert stood all his prickles up very straight and made way for the two rabbits to go in.

"Very good of you to come, Your Highness," he said, and led the way to the little room at the back of the Hall. "I've made this room ready for you. We shall love to have our paws read by the wonderful Bing-Bong." And he bowed again.

Binkle looked round when Herbert had gone out.

"I'll sit in that big chair," he said. "You stand by the door, Flip. Charge a penny a time, remember."

Very soon there came a timid little knock. Flip swung the door open. Outside stood Creeper Mouse.

"Please, I've come to have my paw read," he said nervously, holding out a penny.

"Your Highness! Someone to have his paw read!" called Flip, beginning to enjoy himself.

Binkle put on some big spectacles and glared at Creeper, who stood tremblingly looking at him. He knew Creeper very well, for he was the postman of Oak Tree Town.

"Come here," commanded Binkle, "and hold out your paw."

Creeper put out his tiny little paw. Binkle stared and stared at it.

"Your paw tells me many things," he said. "It tells me that you have five brothers and sisters. You are married, and you —"

"Oh! oh! oh!" squeaked Creeper, lost in wonder. "How clever you are! It's quite true. Does my paw really tell you that?"

"Of course it does," answered Binkle. "Don't interrupt. It tells me that you walk miles and miles every day carrying a heavy bag."

"Yes, yes, I do," squeaked Creeper. "What's in the bag?"

"Your paw will tell me," said Binkle solemnly, bending closely over it. "Let me see – yes, you carry letters. You are a postman."

"Well, did you ever!" exclaimed the astonished mouse, swinging his tail about delightedly. "Oh, Bing-Bong, please tell me what will happen in my future."

Binkle looked at his paw again. "You will go on a long journey, in a ship," he said gravely. "You will carry letters all your life. You will have twenty-nine children."

"No! no!" shrieked Creeper in horror, snatching his paw away. "Twenty-nine children! Why, how would I feed them all? Oh! oh! Twenty-nine children!"

And he rushed out of the room before Binkle could say another word.

Flip began giggling, but Binkle told him to be quiet.

"*Ssh!*" he said. "Creeper will be telling all the others at the Bazaar, and in a minute they'll all want to come and have their paws read. Listen! There's someone now, Flip."

It was Herbert Hedgehog, holding out his penny and looking rather nervous.

"Creeper Mouse says you're wonderful, Your Highness," he said to Binkle. "Could you read *my* paw, please?"

Binkle looked at it solemnly.

"You live in a yellow cottage," he said. "You grow very fine cabbages."

"So I do – so I do," said Herbert, in the greatest astonishment.

"You have many friends," went on Binkle, "but the two who love you best are –"

"Who?" asked Herbert eagerly,

55

wondering if they were Dilly Duck and Sammy Squirrel.

"They are – Flip and Binkle Bunny!" said Binkle, now thoroughly enjoying himself.

Flip's nose went up and down in delight, when he saw the astonishment on Herbert's face.

"My best friends!" echoed Herbert. "Flip and Binkle Bunny! Well, well, well! I must be nicer to them in future."

"I *should*," said Binkle, twirling his whiskers very fast, to hide the smile on his face.

"Tell me some more," begged Herbert. "Tell me about the future."

"Er – if you dig up your biggest cabbages, you *may* find a pot of gold underneath," began Binkle.

"Fancy! Oh, my goodness! Oh, excuse me!" begged Herbert, almost stuttering with excitement. "Pray excuse me! I *do* want to go home straight away and see if I can find that gold."

"Oh no, don't do that," shouted Binkle

in alarm . . . but Herbert was gone.

"Bother!" said Binkle in dismay.

"What do you want to go and say such a silly thing for?" demanded Flip in disgust. "You *know* there's no gold under his cabbages."

"*Ssh!* There's someone else," whispered Binkle, as a knock came at the door.

It was Wily Weasel the policeman! Flip almost fell backwards in fright.

"May I have my paw read?" asked Wily politely.

"Oh – er – yes!" stammered Flip, wishing to goodness he could run away.

Wily went up to Binkle and bowed. Binkle took hold of his paw and glared at it. He didn't like Wily Weasel, for Wily had often told him off for being naughty.

"Your paw does not tell me nice things," he began. "It tells me that you are always hunting others and being unkind to them."

"I have to be," said Wily Weasel

cheerfully. "I'm a policeman! There are lots of rogues about Oak Tree Town, and I have to punish them!"

Binkle decided to change the subject. "You are married," he said, "and you love to smoke a pipe."

"Quite right," said Wily, in a pleased voice. "Now tell me about the future. Shall I get rich?"

"*Never!*" said Binkle firmly. "You'll get poorer and poorer. You'll lose your job. You'll be hunted away from Oak Tree Town. You'll be put in prison. You'll —"

"Ow!" yelled Wily in terror, as he listened to all the awful things Binkle was telling. "Don't tell me any more! I don't want to hear anything else!"

He went hurriedly out of the room, groaning and sighing.

"Ooh, I *did* enjoy that," said Binkle. "That's made up for a good deal of trouble I've had from Wily."

Thick and fast came the knocks on the door, and Binkle was as busy as could be, telling everyone about themselves. As he knew all their pasts and made up their futures, he enjoyed himself thoroughly – till in walked someone he *didn't* know!

He was a badger. He held out his paw to Binkle and waited.

"Er – er – er –" began Binkle. "You live far away from here."

"No, I don't," said the Badger. "I live in the next town."

"That's what I meant," cried Binkle. "Er – er – you are married."

"I'm not!" said the badger indignantly. "You don't know what you're talking about! You're a fraud!"

Just at that moment there came a great hubbub outside the door and it burst open suddenly. Herbert Hedgehog came stamping in, followed by a whole crowd of others.

"I've pulled up all the lovely cabbages in my garden," he wailed, "and there's not a piece of gold anywhere! And all my beautiful cabbages are wasted! You're a fraud, Bing-Bong – that's what you are!"

"Yes, he is," cried the badger. "Why, he told me I was married, and I'm not!"

Wily Weasel strode up to Bing-Bong and glared at him.

"Are you Bing-Bong, or aren't you?" he demanded. "Were all those awful things true that you said were going to happen to me – or not?"

"Oh! oh!" wept Flip. "They weren't true, Wily; he made them up, truly he did!"

Wily turned round and looked at Flip. He grabbed off his queer-shaped hat and the green muffler that hid his chin.

"Oho!" he said, "so it's Flip Bunny, is it? And I suppose Bing-Bong is our old friend Binkle?"

Binkle decided to make the best of it.

"Yes," he said, "I'm Binkle. I only came to the Bazaar to give you a bit of fun. I'm sorry about your cabbages, Herbert. Flip, give him the pennies you've got. He can buy some more."

Everyone stared in astonishment at the red-cloaked rabbit. They could hardly believe it was Binkle who had read their paws. They had so believed in him. For a minute everyone felt angry and probably Flip and Binkle would have been punished – if Creeper Mouse hadn't begun to laugh.

"He told me I'd have twenty-nine children," he squeaked. "Oh dear! Oh dear! And I believed him!"

Then everyone began laughing, and even Wily Weasel joined in.

"I'll let you off *this* time," he said to Binkle. "But next time – you just look out! Go off home, both of you. Give Herbert your pennies to buy more cabbages – and don't let me hear any more of you for a *long* time!"

Flip and Binkle scampered off to Heather Cottage as fast as they could go, very thankful to get off so easily.

And for two weeks Binkle had no more lovely ideas.

Millicent Mary's surprise

Once there was a little girl called Millicent Mary. She had a dear little garden of her own, and in the early spring the very first things that came up were the white snowdrops.

Millicent Mary loved them. She loved the straight green stalks that came up, holding the white bud tightly wrapped up at the top. She liked the two green leaves that sprang up each side. She loved to see the bud slowly unwrap itself, and hang down like a little bell.

But she was always very disappointed because the white bells didn't ring.

"They ought to," said Millicent Mary, and she shook each snowdrop to see if she could make it ring. "Bells like this should ring – they really should! Ring, little snowdrop, ring!"

But not one would ring. Still, Millicent Mary wouldn't give it up. Every morning when she put on her hat and coat and went into the garden, she bent down and shook the snowdrops to see if perhaps today they would say ting-a-ling-a-ling. But they never did.

One day she went to her garden when the snow was on the ground. The snowdrops were buried beneath the snow, and Millicent Mary had to scrape the white snow away very gently to find out where her snowdrops were.

At last all the little white bells were showing. She shook them but no sound came. "Well, you might have rung just a tiny tune to tell me you were grateful to me for scraping the snow away!" said Millicent Mary.

She was just going to stand up and go to the shed to fetch her broom when she saw something rather strange. The snow on the bed nearby seemed to be moving itself – poking itself up as if something was underneath it, wriggling hard.

Millicent Mary was surprised. She was even more surprised when she heard a very tiny voice crying, "Help me! Oh, help me!"

"Goodness gracious!" said the little girl. "There's something buried under the snow just there – and it's got a little tiny voice that speaks!"

She began to scrape away the snow, and her soft, gentle fingers found something small and strange under the white blanket. She pulled out – well, guess what she pulled out!

Yes – you guessed right. It was a tiny pixie, a fairy with frozen silver wings and a little shivering body dressed in a cobweb dress.

"Oh, thank you!" said the pixie in a tiny voice, like a bird cheeping. "I was so tired last night that I crept under a dead leaf and fell asleep. And when I awoke this morning I found a great, thick, cold, white blanket all over me – and I couldn't get it off! Just wait till I catch the person who threw this big blanket all over the garden!"

Millicent Mary laughed. "It's snow!" she said. "It isn't a real blanket. You poor little thing, you feel so cold, you are freezing my fingers. I'm going to take you indoors and get you warm."

She tucked the pixie into her pocket and went indoors. She didn't think she would show the fairy to anyone, because she might vanish – and Millicent Mary didn't want her to do that. It was fun having a pixie, not as big as a doll, to warm before the fire!

The pixie sat on the fender and stretched out her frozen toes to the dancing flames. Millicent Mary took a piece of blue silk out of her mother's rag-bag and gave it to the pixie.

"Wrap this round you for a cloak," she said. "It will keep out the frost when you leave me."

The pixie was delighted. She wrapped the bit of blue silk all round her and pulled it close. "I shall get my needle and thread and make this lovely piece of silk into a proper coat with sleeves and buttons and collar," she said. "You are a dear little girl! I love you. Yes, really I do. Is there anything you would like me to give *you*?"

Millicent Mary thought hard. Then she shook her head. "No," she said at last. "There isn't anything at all, really. I've got all the toys I want. I did badly want a dolls' house, but I had one for Christmas. I don't want any sweets because I've got a tin of barley-sugar. I don't want chocolate biscuits because Mummy bought some yesterday. No – I can't think of anything."

The pixie looked most disappointed. "I do wish you'd try to think of something," she said. "Try hard!"

Millicent Mary thought again. Then she smiled. "Well," she said, "there *is* something I'd simply love – but it needs magic to do it, I think. I'd *love* it if my snowdrops could ring on my birthday, which is on February 13th!"

"Oh, that's easily managed!" said the pixie. "I'll work a spell for it. Let me see – what's your name?"

"Millicent Mary," said the little girl.

"Millicent Mary," said the pixie, writing it down in a tiny notebook. "Birthday, 13th February. Wants snowdrops to ring on that day. All right – I'll see to it! And now goodbye, my dear. I'm deliciously warm with this blue silk. See you again some day. Don't forget to listen to your snowdrops on February 13th!"

She skipped up into the air, spread her silvery wings, and flew straight out of the top of the window. Millicent Mary couldn't help feeling tremendously excited. Her birthday would soon be here – and just imagine the snowdrops ringing!

Won't she love to shake each tiny white bell, and hear it ring ting-a-ling-a-ling, ting-a-ling-a-ling! Is *your* name Millicent Mary, by any chance, and is *your* birthday on 13th February? If it is, the snowdrops will ring for you too, without a doubt – so don't forget to shake each little white bell on that day, and hear the tinkling sound they make. What a lovely surprise for all the Millicent Marys!

The cat who flew away

There was once a cat who couldn't be trusted. His name was Whiskers, because he had such fine strong whiskers growing out at each side of his face.

He stole anything and everything he could. He jumped on to the kitchen table directly the cook's back was turned, and jumped off again with a tart, or a kipper, or a sausage in his mouth. Then out of the window he sprang like a flash, before Cook had time to see what he had got.

Whiskers didn't mind what he ate. He was always hungry, and he enjoyed bits of sugar, currants, bread, lemonade, tea leaves, and anything else you can think of that can be found lying on the kitchen table. Nothing seemed to cure him of his wicked ways, and he was so clever that he was hardly ever caught.

Then one day he ate something that gave him a very funny feeling. He didn't know what it was, but he licked it up till it was all gone. Cook had been making cakes, and she had left the self-raising flour on the table. She had gone to change her dress, and there was nobody in the kitchen when Whiskers found the open bag, and began to lick up the flour. It went up his nose and made him sneeze, but he didn't mind a little thing like that.

His whiskers became white with the flour, and his black fur was flecked with the powdery stuff. He went on and on eating the flour, and only stopped when he heard Cook coming downstairs. Then he leapt out of the window, and as he went, he heard Cook shout out angrily.

"If that thief of a cat hasn't gone and snuffed up the self-raising flour!" she cried. "Well, it won't do him any good, I'm certain of that!"

Whiskers went and sat on a wall in the sun, and washed himself. It was while he was washing himself that he felt so funny. He stopped washing himself to think about the strange feeling that was coming over him. He felt as if he were suddenly very swollen and very light – rather like a balloon must feel when it is being blown up.

You see, the self-raising flour was beginning to act on him, just as it acts on cakes and bread. It makes them rise in the oven, and become nice and light to eat. Whiskers had sat himself down in the hot sun, and the flour was beginning to make him very light too.

"Whiskers and tails!" said the cat in alarm, digging his claws hard into the wall. "What's happening to me? I shall be floating up in the air in a minute, I feel so light and airy!"

And all at once he rose into the air! Up he went, clawing at the air, wondering whatever was going to happen. The sparrows who had been watching him from a nearby tree began to shout in surprise to each other.

"Chirrup, chirrup! Look at the cat! If he takes to flying in the air like us, we shan't have a chance to escape! Chirrup!"

They flew away in alarm and told the old jackdaw who lived in the church tower. He came at once to see the marvellous sight of a cat flying through the air, and when he saw poor old Whiskers, he cawed in delight.

"He's not flying!" he said. "He's gone up in the air like those round balloons do that the children play with. Oh my, what a game! Come on, boys, and we'll chase him!"

The sparrows were still too frightened to go near Whiskers, so the jackdaw fetched his friends the rooks, and all the

great black birds flew after Whiskers, who was still floating along in the air, getting higher and higher every minute.

He was very much afraid when he saw the birds coming after him, because he remembered how often he had chased some of them. He was just wondering what to do about it, when he floated over a smoking chimney, and the smoke got into his nose and eyes, and made him sneeze violently.

"Caw!" cried a rock, and pecked at his tail.

"Ka-kack!" said the jackdaw, and pulled out one of his hairs. Whiskers couldn't do anything, because as fast as he tried to claw at the birds, they dodged away, and pecked him somewhere else.

Whiskers rose higher and higher, and soon he was so high that the jackdaw and the rooks left him. He came to where the swallows and the martins were flying very high up, looking for insects. When they saw him they flew off in alarm, but one swallow saw that he was the cat who had frightened three of her babies the day before, and she flew at him and pecked off the end of one of his fine whiskers.

Then the others came up, and some swifts screeched so loudly in his ear that he jumped with fright, and found himself even higher than before.

Up he went, until he came to where an eagle soared round and round and round. Now Whiskers had never seen an eagle close to, and he had no idea what this enormous creature was. The eagle was astonished to see such a strange animal floating so high and swooped downwards to see him closely.

"This might be food for my eaglets," thought the great bird, circling round the frightened cat. He was just going to pounce when the self-raising flour stopped acting, and Whiskers found himself sinking quickly downwards. The eagle watched in astonishment, and decided not to catch him after all.

Down went Whiskers, and down, past the astonished swallows, and through a flock of alarmed starlings, who flew at him, and made him blink his eyes in fright.

Faster and faster, faster and faster! Then suddenly splash! He fell into the pond of water at the bottom of his own garden, and sent the ducks waddling helter-skelter away, quacking loudly. All except one duck – and she had a brood of little ones nearby, so she rushed angrily at Whiskers as he spluttered out of the water, and gave him such a punch with her beak that he fell back into the pond again.

Poor old Whiskers! He dragged himself off, and found a warm place in the sun to dry himself. It took him quite two hours to get dry, and all the sparrows flew down to a nearby tree, and made rude remarks to him.

And perhaps you won't be surprised to hear that Whiskers is a cat who *can* be trusted now. He never steals *anything*, and the cook can't think why! But *we* could tell her, couldn't we!

The Gossamer Elf

E verybody knew the Gossamer Elf. She was the cleverest dressmaker in the whole of Fairyland. You should have seen the dresses and cloaks she made!

"I think her autumn clothes are the best," said Winks. "She made me a lovely dress last October of a red creeper leaf. I went to lots of parties in it."

"She made me a cloak out of a pair of beech leaves," said Feefo. "It was a golden cloak, the prettiest I ever had."

"Her stitches are the finest I ever saw," said Tiptoe. "Well – they're so fine I can't see them! Once I thought

that the Gossamer Elf didn't sew our frocks at all, but just made them by magic. She doesn't though; I've seen her sewing away with a tiny, tiny needle."

"Ah, but have you seen her thread?" said Winks. "It's so fine and so strong that once she's put a stitch into a dress it never comes undone."

"What does she use for thread?" said Feefo. "I'd like to get some. I'll go and ask her."

So she went to call on the Gossamer Elf. But the Elf was out. She had left her door open and Feefo went inside. On a shelf she saw reels upon reels — but they were all empty. Not one reel had any thread on it. How strange!

Soon the Gossamer Elf came in. Feefo ran to her. "I've come to ask you something. Where do you get your fine thread? I can't see any on your reels."

The Gossamer Elf smiled. "No — my reels are all empty now," she said. "But soon they will be filled again with the finest, silkiest thread. I always get my thread at this time of year, you know."

"Where from?" asked Feefo. "Can I get some too? Do let me. Take me with you and I'll buy some."

"I don't buy it," said the Elf. "Yes, you can come with me if you like. I'm starting out tomorrow morning at dawn. You can carry some of my empty reels with you. That will be a help."

So Feefo and the Gossamer Elf set out at dawn. They went to the fields. It was a lovely morning, and the sun shone softly from a blue sky.

"It's gossamer time now," said the Elf. "Did you know that? Soon the air will be full of fine silken threads that will stretch across the fields everywhere. See – you can spy some already, gleaming in the sun."

Feefo looked. Yes – she could see some fine, long threads stretching from the hedge above high up into the air. Soon there would be plenty of them.

"But what are those silky threads?" said Feefo in wonder. "Where do they come from? Who makes them?"

"Climb up the hedge with me and I'll show you," said the Elf. "Some very small friends of mine make them. We'll watch them."

They climbed up the hedge together, using the prickles on the wild rose stems as steps. They soon got high up in the hedge. Then Feefo saw around her many tiny spiders – young ones, not much more than babies.

Some stood on leaves, some clung to stems, and all of them were doing the same thing. They were sending out long silken threads from underneath their bodies.

"They have their silk spinnerets there," said the Elf. "Big spiders have too. They take the thread from their spinnerets. Watch that tiny spider. See the long thread coming out, and waving in the air?"

"Oh, yes," said Feefo, in surprise. She saw dozens of tiny spiders all doing the same thing. "But why are they all doing this, Elf? It seems very strange to me. They are not spinning webs."

"No, they are going out into the world to seek their fortunes," said the Elf. "Each baby spider wants to leave the place where he was born. He wants to journey far away and find his own place to live. So he is sending out a long, long thread into the air – and then, when he has a long enough line, he will let the wind take him off into the air with his gossamer thread – and, like a tiny parachutist, he will soar over the world, and then drop gently to ground."

"Goodness me!" said Feefo, astonished. "Look, there goes one, Elf! Away he goes on the wind."

The tiny spider had let go his hold of the leaf, and now, swinging gently on the end of his gossamer thread, he let himself be carried away on the breeze, exactly like a tiny parachutist. Feefo and the Elf watched him soaring away, until he could no longer be seen.

"They're all doing it, all the baby spiders!" cried Feefo in delight. "Oh, look at them swinging away on their threads. The wind blows the threads away and the spiders go with them!"

They watched the curious sight for a little while. Then Feefo turned to the Elf. "But, Elf," she said, "surely you don't take their threads away from the tiny spiders? That would be a most unkind thing to do."

"Of course I don't," said the Elf. "How could you think I'd do that? No – once the spiders have made their journey and landed safely somewhere, they don't want their threads any more. So I collect them on my reels, you see. I wind them up carefully, and soon have all my reels full for my year's work."

"Well, what a good idea," cried Feefo. "Look – here comes a spider from far away; see him swinging down on the end of his line? Here he is, just beside us. Little spider, what an adventure you've had!"

"May I take your thread please, if you don't want it any more?" asked the Gossamer Elf politely. "Oh, thank you. What a nice long one!"

She began to wind the gossamer round and round her reel. Soon the reel was full. The spider ran off to find himself a nice new home under a leaf. Maybe he would catch plenty of flies there, he thought. Soon he would spin a fine web, and wait for his dinner to come along and fly into it.

Another spider landed a little farther down. Feefo ran to him. As soon as he had cast off his gossamer she began to wind it round and round the reel she carried. "What fun this is!" she thought. "Now I know why the Gossamer Elf has her name. How clever she is to think of this idea!"

Day after day, early in the morning, Feefo and the Gossamer Elf came out together and waited for the adventuring spiders to land near them on their gossamer lines. Soon they had dozens and dozens of reels full of the fine silken thread.

"There. We've got enough!" said the Elf at last. "Now I shall wait for the leaves to change colour, and soon I shall be hard at work again making winter dresses and cloaks and sewing them with the gossamer thread given me by the tiny spiders. I shall be very busy indeed this winter!"

So she is. She is making coats of blackberry leaves, crimson, yellow and pink; frocks of golden hazel leaves, trimmed with berries, and cloaks of brilliant cherry leaves. You should see them! But you can't see her stitches — they are made of the gossamer from the spiders.

Have you ever seen it? You really must. You can take some too, if you want, for the spiders won't need it again.

The day the Princess came

"The Princess is coming to visit our village!" shouted Bron the brownie, racing through the streets, waving a letter. "Next week! Hurray! She wants to have tea in one of our cottages! Hurray!"

Well, what an excitement! A meeting was held at once, and all the villagers went to it, of course.

"Now, we must vote for the prettiest, best-kept cottage in our village," said Bron, importantly. "All our cottages are pretty, but not all of them are tidy and clean and well-kept inside. The Princess must have tea in the one that is best inside as well as outside."

So all the villagers voted on bits

of paper and put down the name of the cottage they thought to be the best for the Princess to have tea in.

"I'll count the votes," said Bron, and he did. He looked up, puzzled. "*Two* cottages have exactly the same number of votes!" he said. "Cherry Cottage, where Dame Twinkle lives – and Apple Cottage, where old Mother Quickfeet lives. Exactly the same number of votes each!"

"Well – let the Princess choose which cottage she will have tea in when she comes!" called out Pippitty the pixie. "*We* can't choose. Both cottages are beautiful, inside and out."

So it was left like that – and dear me, how Mother Quickfeet and Dame Twinkle set to work to make their cottages shine and sparkle!

Their gardens were lovely, full of hollyhocks and cornflowers and marigolds and sweet-peas, and there wasn't a weed to be seen. Dame Twinkle got Bron to whitewash her cottage and Mother Quickfeet got Pippitty to paint her shutters a pretty blue.

And dear me, what a lot of work went on inside! Each cottage had just two rooms, a bedroom and a parlour. Up went new curtains, each carpet was beaten till it could have cried, and the floors were polished till they were like mirrors. New cushion-covers were made, flowers were set in every corner, the windows were cleaned over and over again, and the smell of freshly baked pies came out of the open doors of the cottages, and made everyone wish they could go and taste them!

That was the day before the Princess was to visit the village. People came and peeped inside the two cottages, wondering which one the Princess would choose.

"I *think* she'll choose Mother Quickfeet's," said Bron. "She has such a pretty wallpaper, so fresh and flowery."

"Ah, but Dame Twinkle has a

rocking-chair," said Pippitty. "I'm sure the Princess would like to sit in that rocking-chair."

Now that night something happened. The cottage next door to Mother Quickfeet's caught fire. It was a little thatched cottage, and soon the straw roof was sending up big flames to the sky. What a to-do!

"Old Man Surly's cottage is burning!" cried Dame Twinkle, when she went out to take in her washing. Just then Mrs Surly rushed into her own garden and called out loudly.

"We can't save the cottage. My children are frightened. So are the cat and the dog. Please, please will you and Mother Quickfeet take us in for the night?"

Then Mother Quickfeet ran out into *her* garden. Dear, dear, what a to-do! Nothing would save that old cottage now. Well, it was tumbling down anyway, and it was all Mr Surly's fault for never doing anything to put it right!

"You can all go to your uncle's," said Mother Quickfeet. "He's got a nice big house, and he'll take you in."

"But it's night-time, and he lives such a long way away," wept Mrs Surly. "And my baby is ill. Oh, please do let us rest in your two cottages tonight, Mother Quickfeet and Dame Twinkle."

Now there were three boys and girls in the Surly family besides the baby – and, alas, they were not very well brought-up children. They were rough and rather rude. As for the dog, he was a dreadful chewer, and everyone shooed him away if they saw him because he would chew up carpets or shoes or books – anything he came across!

"We can't have you," said Mother Quickfeet, firmly. "It's quite impossible. Surely you know that Mother Twinkle and I are hoping to have the Princess to tea tomorrow, and have got our cottages simply beautiful? No – you go to your uncle's. It's your own fault that the cottage has caught fire. You don't sweep the chimney often enough."

Mrs Surly began to cry. The baby howled. The dog barked. Mr Surly growled, and picked up the baby's cradle, which he had managed to save.

"All right," he said. "We'll go. Maybe we can find someone kinder than you, with your talk of beautiful cottages and lovely princesses!"

The little company set off gloomily down the lane. They passed Mother Quickfeet's cottage, and she kept the door shut fast! They passed Dame Twinkle's, too – but before they had gone very far she was out of her door and at the gate calling loudly.

"Mrs Surly! You can come in here. I can't bear to let you walk all that way to your uncle's in the dark of night. Come along in, all of you!"

Mother Quickfeet opened her door. "*Well!*" she said, "fancy having that rough, bad-mannered family to stay with you the night before the Princess arrives! You must be mad!"

"Well – perhaps I am," said Dame Twinkle. "I can't help it. I just feel so sorry for them all. And anyway they'll be gone tomorrow morning and I can easily clear up after them and make things nice again. Are you sure you won't have one or two of the children tonight, Mother Quickfeet? They'll make such a crowd in my cottage."

"Certainly *not*," said Mother Quickfeet and she slammed her door quickly.

Soon all the Surly family was in Cherry Cottage – and dear me, they certainly filled every corner! What with the baby, three other children, Mr and Mrs Surly, *and* the cat and dog, there didn't seem anywhere to sit or even to stand!

Dame Twinkle made them as comfortable as she could. They were all hungry, so she gave them all the pies and cakes and jam sandwiches she had made for the next day.

"I can easily make some more," she thought. "Oh dear – that dog is chewing my new rug. Shoo, dog, shoo!"

The dog shooed away, and began to chew a cushion. The cat leapt up on the mantelpiece and knocked down the clock – smash!

The three children squashed into the lovely rocking-chair and rocked hard. Creak, creak, crash! One of the rockers broke and down went all the children.

"Oh dear – my lovely rocking-chair," said Dame Twinkle, sadly. "Oh, Mrs Surly, *don't* let the baby pull my flowers out of that vase!"

But the baby did, and after that he crawled to the coal-scuttle, and threw bits of coal all over the place! The dog chewed the bits, and then when anyone walked across the room, crunch-crunch went the bits of chewed-up coal under their feet!

Mr Surly lighted his pipe. Goodness gracious, what a smoke he made, and how horrid it smelt! Mother Twinkle almost cried. Would the smell of smoke have gone from the room before the Princess came?

Next morning Mother Quickfeet looked into Dame Twinkle's cottage. My goodness, what a mess! A dirty floor, torn cushions, a chewed-up carpet, a broken rocking-chair, and everything in a mess and a muddle!

Mother Quickfeet didn't say a word. She went back to her own trim and tidy cottage, smiling. Aha! Dame Twinkle wouldn't *dream* of inviting the Princess in now. That was quite certain. She would come to tea with Mother Quickfeet, in Apple Cottage.

After breakfast Mr Surly fetched a big hand barrow from the greengrocer's. He piled on to it the few things saved from the fire. The baby was set on it, too, and the little family set off down the lane to go to their uncle's.

"Goodbye, dear, kind Dame Twinkle," said Mrs Surly, hugging her. "I do wish I could stay and help you to clean up, but if we don't start off now we'll never get there. I shall *never* forget your kindness."

Poor Dame Twinkle. She looked round her little cottage, and almost cried. So dirty. So untidy. So many things broken – even her beloved rocking-chair. Could she ever get things straight in time?

She tried her best. She scrubbed the floor, and when it was dry she polished it. She washed the cushions and mended them. She put the broken clock away. She called in Pippitty to mend the rocking-chair, but he said it would take a whole week.

"What a mess your place is in," he said. "It was very kind of you to take in that poor family – but, oh dear, how sad just before the Princess was arriving! I'm *sure* she would have chosen you to have tea with, Dame Twinkle."

Dame Twinkle looked round the room sadly. "I shan't bother about it any more," she said. "No matter how hard I work I won't have time to get it nice again now. Mother Quickfeet must have the Princess to tea – her cottage really does look lovely."

So Dame Twinkle didn't try to do much more to her cottage. She was tired out with her disturbed night so, after dinner, she changed her dress, and put on her best one, so that she could stand at her front gate and wave to the Princess, when she came.

Cloppetty-cloppetty-clop! That was the sound of horses' hooves. The Princess was coming, hurrah, hurrah, hurrah! All the villagers lined the road and shouted and cheered, for they loved the beautiful, kind-hearted princess.

Along came the carriage, what a beauty! And there was the princess, lovelier than ever, a shining crown on her golden hair. She bowed this way and that, and looked just as pleased as the cheering people.

"Your Royal Highness, Mother

Quickfeet, whose cottage is the prettiest and best of all, begs you to take a cup of tea with her," said Bron the brownie, bowing low. He guided the carriage horses to Apple Cottage. At the gate stood Mother Quickfeet, looking very grand indeed in plum-coloured silk, smiling all over her face.

"Wait," said the Princess. "It is *Cherry* Cottage I want, not Apple Cottage."

"No, no," said Bron, hurriedly. "You're making a mistake, Your Highness. It's *Apple* Cottage!"

"Listen to me," said the Princess, in a little, high voice that everyone could hear. "On my way here I met a little family. The man was pushing a hand barrow, and a baby was crying in the middle of it. I stopped and asked them what they were doing and where they were going. And do you know what they said?"

"What?" asked everyone, crowding close.

"They said they had lost their house in a fire last night and had asked Mother Quickfeet at Apple Cottage to take them in – and she wouldn't. But they said that Dame Twinkle, at Cherry Cottage, called after them and took them all in, every one!"

"Good old Dame Twinkle!" shouted Pippitty.

"Mrs Surly told me they had made a mess of her beautiful cottage, and she said she was very sorry because she knew Dame Twinkle wanted me to go to have tea with her," went on the Princess. "Where *is* this kind Dame Twinkle?"

"Here she is, here she is!" yelled Bron the brownie, in excitement, and showed the Princess where the kind old woman was standing wonderingly at her front gate.

"Oh, please!" Dame Twinkle said, half-scared. "Oh, please, dear Bron, don't ask the Princess in to tea at my house. It's in *such* a mess!"

"Dear Dame Twinkle, I'm not coming to tea with you today!" called the little Princess. "I know how horrid it is to have visitors when your house is untidy. So I'm going to take you home to tea with *me*, back to the palace. Will you come?"

What an honour for Dame Twinkle! No one in the whole village had *ever* gone to tea with a Princess before.

And there was Dame Twinkle stepping into the royal carriage, blushing red, hardly able to speak a word!

"Next week I'll come and have tea with *you*, Dame Twinkle," said the Princess, loud enough for Mother Quickfeet to hear. "Not because you have a pretty cottage, which is a common enough thing – but because you've a warm, kind heart, and that's quite rare! Now – are you quite comfortable? And do you like meringues for tea, because I know we've got some at the palace?"

Nobody heard what Dame Twinkle answered, because the carriage drove off at that moment, clippitty-clop-clop. Everyone cheered again. They didn't mind the Princess paying such a short visit, because she would be back again the next week. Hurrah!

"Good old Dame Twinkle – she deserves a treat," cried Bron. "Three cheers, everyone!"

And every single person joined in – except Mother Quickfeet, who had gone quietly back into her beautiful cottage to cry.

Oh dear – what could she do now? Well – she could go and tidy up Dame Twinkle's cottage, and bake her some pies to welcome her when she came back.

Do you suppose she did? I do hope so.

Mollie's mud-pies

It was very hot, so hot that Mollie wore only a swimsuit. It was nearly summer, and Mummy said if it was so hot now, whatever would it be like in the middle of summer.

"It's nice," said Mollie, who liked wearing almost nothing. She didn't even wear shoes in the garden. "I like it, Mummy. I do wish we were by the sea, then I could swim."

"Well, I'll tell you what I will do," said her mother. "I will water you each night before you go to bed!"

"Water me!" said Mollie, in surprise. "What do you mean, Mummy?"

"Just what I say," said Mummy. "I'll fill a can with half-warm water, and

then water you before you go to bed.
That will be fun for you."

"Oh, *yes*," said Mollie in delight. "I
should love that."

She played in the hot garden. The
grass looked yellow, not green.
Everywhere was dried up and dusty.
Mollie wondered if the birds had any
puddles to drink from. They must be
thirsty now, with all the puddles dried
up. So she filled a little bowl with water,
and set it out on the grass. It was fun to
see the birds coming to drink from it.

"They drink so sweetly," said Mollie.
"They dip in their beaks, and then hold
their heads back, Mummy, and let the
water run down their throats."

When the evening came, Mummy
filled a big watering-can with half-
warm water, and called Mollie."Come
and have your watering!"

"Will it make me grow, like the
flowers?" cried Mollie, dancing about.
Mummy tipped up the can. Mollie gave
a squeal. Although the water was not

cold, it felt cold on her hot little body. She danced about, squeaking with excitement and joy.

"The water's made a nice muddy patch on the path," she cried. "Look, my toes are brown and muddy with dancing in it."

"You'll have to wash them well," said Mummy, filling the can again. "Come along – one more watering and you must go to bed."

The patch of path was indeed wet and muddy after the second can of water had been poured all over Mollie. "If it's wet tomorrow, I shall make little mud-pies of it," said Mollie.

It was still muddy the next day. After breakfast Mollie went to the mud and dabbled her fingers in it. "I shall make little pies and cakes of mud, and set them in the sun to dry," she thought. "That will be a nice game to play."

Mummy called her. "If you want to play that dirty game you must wear an overall over that nice clean swimsuit. Come along."

Mollie ran indoors. When she came out again she found someone else in her mud-patch! It was a little bird with a touch of white at the foot of his dark, long tail, and underneath his body. He stared at Mollie, and then scraped up some mud in his beak.

"Oh!" said Mollie, pleased. "Are you making mud-pies too? I never knew a bird liked playing with mud before. Do play with me."

The little bird gave a twitter, filled his beak quite full, and then suddenly darted into the air on curving wings.

Mollie saw that he had a forked tail behind him.

"I wish he hadn't gone," she thought. "It would have been fun to play with him. I suppose he has taken the mud to make mud-pies somewhere else."

Suddenly the little bird came back again. He looked at Mollie, and she looked at him. He wondered if Mollie was the kind of child to throw stones at him, or to shout and frighten him away.

But she wasn't. She was like you. She liked birds, and wanted them to stay close to her so that she could watch them and make friends with them.

She sat quite still and watched him. He went to the mud again, and began to scrape up some more. Then another bird, exactly like him, flew down, and he began to dabble in it as well. Mollie was delighted.

"Everyone is making mud-pies this morning," she said. "Gracious – here's another! How busy they all are in my muddy patch. I'll get busy too."

Once the birds had made up their minds that Mollie was a friend, they became very busy indeed. They filled their little beaks with mud time after time, and then flew away round the house. Mollie wondered where they went. They kept coming and going all the morning.

"Funny little mud-pie birds," she said to them. "Do you bake your mud-pies up on the roof somewhere? I bake mine here, look!"

The hot sun baked her pies beautifully. She put them on a plate out of her tea-set and took them in to her mummy.

"Have a mud-pie?" she said. "They are lovely. And, oh, Mummy, the mud-pie birds have played in the mud with me all morning. They were sweet."

Mummy was surprised. "Mud-pie birds! Whatever do you mean?"

"Well, they came and played with my mud and took some away to make mud-pies with. I expect they baked them up on the roof," said Mollie.

Mummy thought it was a little tale of Mollie's. She pretended to eat Mollie's mud-pie, and then offered Mollie a bun from the oven.

"I've been baking too," she said. "Have a hot bun? And now I think you had better stop playing with the mud and wash yourself."

"The mud is gone now," said Mollie. "The sun has baked it hard."

The little birds didn't come into the garden any more that day. "I suppose they only came for the mud," thought Mollie. "Well, if Mummy waters me again tonight there will be more mud tomorrow for us all to play with."

There was – a nice big patch – and down came the little birds again, to scrape up the mud. Mollie was so pleased.

"It's nice to have you to play with me," she said to the busy little birds. "But I really wish you would tell me what you do with your mud."

They twittered a little song to her, high and sweet, but she didn't understand what they said. They flew to and from the mud all morning, till the sun dried it up.

"Mummy, why do the mud-pie birds take my mud?" asked Mollie. "I do want to know. I didn't know that birds like mud so much."

Her daddy was there, and he looked up from his newspaper. "What's all this about mud-pie birds?" he asked. So Mollie told him.

"Ah," he said. "Now I know what birds you mean. Your mud-pie birds are house-martins, cousins of the pretty swallows we see flying high in the air all summer."

"House-martins!" said Mollie. "*I* should call them mud-martins. What do they do with my mud?"

"Come with me and I'll show you," said Daddy. He took Mollie's hand, and led her upstairs. They went into her

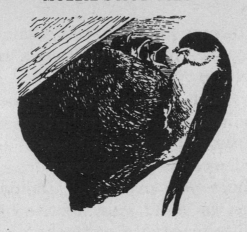

bedroom. Daddy went to the window and opened it wide.

"Now look out of your window, above it, to the edge of the roof overhead," he said. "Tell me what you see."

Mollie leaned out, and looked up. She gave a cry. "Oh, Daddy! The mud-pie birds are there. They are making something of my mud. What is it?"

"It's a nest," said Daddy. "The house-martins don't use dead leaves and twigs and moss for their nests as most birds do. They make them of mud. They fetch beakfuls of mud, and plaster it against the wall, gradually building it out till they have made a fine nest of mud, with a hole to get in and out. There's the hole in that nest. Look!"

As Mollie watched, one of the little birds flew up with his beak full of mud from somewhere, and pressed it against the edge of his nest.

"There you are," said Daddy. "He brings wet mud, and it dries hard in the sun, making a perfectly good nest for his little wife to lay her eggs in, and have her young ones."

"Oh, Daddy! Fancy making a nest of my mud, the mud that was made when Mummy watered me each evening," said Mollie in delight. "I couldn't think why the mud-birds came to make mud-pies. I did not know they were making mud-nests – and over my bedroom window, too, tucked under the edge of the roof! I shall hear them calling and twittering to each other all day long. Look – there's another nest farther along. You won't pull them down, will you?"

"Of course not!" said Daddy, who was fond of birds. "They can nest there in peace and happiness, out of reach of the cats. Later on we shall see their young ones popping their heads out of the holes in the mud-nests."

And so they did! The house-martins laid eggs in their strange mud-nests, and in a few weeks' time Mollie saw three or four tiny feathery heads popping out of the hole in the nest above her window, waiting for the father and mother to come back with flies to feed them.

Later still the little birds flew into the sky with their mother and father, learning how to dart and soar and glide, and how to catch the hundreds of insects that flew in the air. Daddy said they did a great deal of good, because the flies were a pest.

And then one day they were all gone. Mollie looked into the sky and they were not there.

"They've gone away south, where it

is warmer," said Daddy. "There will be plenty of insects for them to eat there. Our winter is coming and they do not like that."

"I don't want them to go away," said Mollie sadly.

"Well, they will be back again in the spring," said Daddy. "And, Mollie, if the weather is hot and dry again when they come back, you must make a muddy patch once more, and they will come to it, and build their nest again over your window. They love to come back to exactly the same place, if they can."

So, of course, Mollie is going to watch for them when the spring comes. You must watch too, and if we have hot and dry weather in May, when the mud-pie birds want to build their nests, you can do as Mollie did – make a muddy patch for them, and watch them fly down to it to fill their beaks.

Maybe they will build a mud-nest over your window, too. That really would be fun, wouldn't it?

Brer Rabbit goes fishing

One winter's night Brer Rabbit thought he would go fishing. He went and called on Brer Terrapin to ask him if he would go too.

"I'm taking my boat," said Brer Rabbit. "I'm going to row right across the river to the other side, to a place where there's plenty of fish. You come, too, Brer Terrapin. We'll catch some good fish for breakfast this hungry weather."

"Do you mind if my old uncle comes, too?" said Brer Terrapin. "Stick your head out, Uncle, and say 'Howdy' to Brer Rabbit."

"Howdy-do!" said Brer Terrapin's old uncle, shooting his neck out suddenly

from under his big shell.

"Howdy!" said Brer Rabbit. "Yes, bring your uncle too, Brer Terrapin. Plenty of room in my boat!"

"Brrrrrr!" said Brer Terrapin as they all three went to find Brer Rabbit's boat tied up by the river. "It's freezing cold, Brer Rabbit. Good thing I've got no whiskers, or they'd freeze up like icicles! You be careful of yours!"

They all got into the boat and Brer Rabbit rowed right across to the other side of the river. "You be careful, Brer Rabbit," said Brer Terrapin, peering over the edge of the boat. "Brer Wolf lives near here, and he likes to fish about here, too. You be careful he doesn't catch you."

Just as he spoke there came a bellow from the bank. It was old Brer Wolf!

"Hey, Brer Rabbit! What are you doing in my bit of fishing-water? You get out!"

Brer Rabbit drew in his oars and threw out a small anchor.

"We'll anchor here," he said to the terrapins, not taking a bit of notice of Brer Wolf's yells. "Don't you worry about all that shouting. It's just noise and nothing else. Brer Wolf's boat has got a hole in it, so he can't come after us. We'll fish here and see what we get."

Well, they caught a whole lot of fish, and Brer Wolf got quite hoarse with shouting at them and telling them to get out of his bit of fishing-water. But pretty soon he got tired of that and went back to his home nearby.

Then Brer Rabbit suddenly noticed that he couldn't jerk his line out of the water. What was happening? He peered over the edge of the boat in the moonlight – and what a shock he got! The river was freezing fast!

"My, my!" said Brer Rabbit, startled. "We'd better get back before the river's quite frozen. It must be a bitter cold night tonight."

But the boat wouldn't move! It was stuck fast in the ice. The oars broke through the ice, but Brer Rabbit couldn't use them. He looked at the terrapins in fright.

"What'll we do? The water's frozen! We're stuck!"

"That's bad," said Brer Terrapin. "See if the ice will hold you, Brer Rabbit. Then maybe we can slide back."

Very soon the ice was hard enough to hold them. But poor Brer Rabbit couldn't go a step without falling down – and as for the terrapins, their legs just slid helplessly on the ice, and they didn't get anywhere at all!

"Brer Wolf will see what's happened when daylight comes!" said Brer Rabbit, with a groan. "He'll put on his skates and skate over the ice to the boat – and maybe he'll have rabbit-and-terrapin pie for his dinner!"

The river was frozen even harder by the morning. Brer Wolf was surprised to see it covered with ice when he peeped out of his window next morning. Aha! There was Brer Rabbit's boat stuck fast in the frozen river.

"Just wait till I get my skates on and I'll catch you all right, Brer Rabbit!" yelled Brer Wolf.

Brer Rabbit watched Brer Wolf come

down to the bank of the frozen river. He watched him put on his skates.

"If only I had some skates!" he groaned. "I'd skate out of sight in two shakes of a duck's tail! But none of us can escape because we can't even *stand* on this slippery ice!"

Then Brer Terrapin's old uncle spoke up. "Maybe I know a way to get us all free," he said. "Now see, Brer Rabbit. Put me out of the boat on to my back – and Brer Terrapin, too."

"What's the use of *that*?" said Brer Rabbit.

"Then after that you get out, too," said Brer Terrapin's uncle. "And you put one foot on my underside and the other on Brer Terrapin's – and we'll catch hold of your toes hard. And you can skate away on us, right to the other side of the river. We'll be your skates, Brer Rabbit; our shells will slide as fast as anything!"

What an idea! Brer Rabbit dropped them on to the ice, upside down, side by side. He hopped overboard himself and put a hind foot on each. The terrapins held his feet firmly in their clawed feet.

Just as Brer Wolf came skating over the ice, Brer Rabbit skated off, too, with the two upside-down terrapins for his skates! He went like the wind – and Brer Wolf was so astonished that his feet caught in one another and over he went, higgledy-piggledy, on the ice.

"Take a few lessons, Brer Wolf, take a few lessons!" yelled out Brer Rabbit, and came to a stop at the opposite bank. The terrapins let go his feet and he leapt off. He put them the right way up, and they scrambled down the nearest hole.

"Like one of my fish, Brer Wolf?" shouted Brer Rabbit, and threw one at Brer Wolf. It hit him smack on the nose – and off went wicked Brer Rabbit with his string of fish, laughing fit to kill himself. And I guess that he and the two terrapins feasted on a fine fish-pie that night!

The bonnet dame

Once upon a time, I couldn't tell you how long ago, there lived a strange old woman, who was half a witch. She was always called the bonnet dame, because she got her living by making little white bonnets for babies.

Now the strange thing about Dame Bonnet was that the older she got, the smaller she grew. She was thin and brown, like a bent twig, and her voice was as husky as two leaves rubbing one against the other, but her hands were still as nimble as ever, and she made her white bonnets even more beautifully.

But of course, as she grew smaller, so did the bonnets she made, and after a while mothers didn't buy them any more, for they didn't fit their babies. Then Dame Bonnet went to Brownie-Town and lived there, for the brownies had nice small babies, and her bonnets fitted them well.

Then she grew smaller still and her bonnets no longer fitted even the brownie babies. So she went to Elf-land and there her bonnets fitted the grown-up elves, for they are small creatures, and when Dame Bonnet grew even smaller it didn't matter because then her lovely bonnets fitted the elf babies. So she stayed there quite a long time and was very happy indeed.

Then she grew so very small that the bonnets fitted nobody at all. She tried here and she tried there – the gnomes were far too big in the head; the goblins were the wrong shape, and even the very smallest dwarfs were too large about the head. So Dame Bonnet made no money at all, and began to shrivel away like a dead leaf.

Then one day she met some tiny creatures, slim and sweet, dressed in green. Their heads were bare, and the wind blew their hair about untidily. Dame Bonnet looked at them and wondered if her white bonnets would fit them.

"Who are you?" she asked. "I don't think I've seen you before."

"We are the little Fair Maids," said the small creatures, "half-fairies, half-flowers. We live in the woods, and we are always trying to find a sheltered spot, because the wind blows our hair about so much. He is very rough with us, and we do not like him."

The wind swept down and whipped the tiny creatures' hair about their gentle faces. Dame Bonnet watched, and then she offered them her small white bonnets – so small now that the stitches in them could not be seen!

"Wear these!" she said, in her husky voice. "You need not pay me. Only let me keep near to you, Fair Maids, and

talk to me sometimes. I am an old, old woman, and I would so much like your youthful company to cheer me."

The Fair Maids tried on the small white bonnets, and to their great delight they fitted most beautifully. "Thank you!" they said gratefully. "Please do keep near us if you like, Dame Bonnet. We shall love to talk to you."

Well, my dears, the Fair Maids still wear the tiny white bonnets made by the old half-witch. You can see them any day in February in gardens and woods, half-fairies, half-flowers – small, fairy-like snowdrops, standing in little groups together. And not far off you will perhaps see something that looks just like a shrivelled brown leaf. It *may* be a dead leaf, of course, but if it scuttles away fast when you bend down, you'll know what it really is – old Dame Bonnet herself!